# DUMP
## the Orange Orangutan

## Written by Joshua Dwyer
### Illustrations by Sarah LaFayette

Balboa Press books may be ordered through booksellers or by contacting:

Balboa Press
A Division of Hay House
1663 Liberty Drive
Bloomington, IN 47403
www.balboapress.com
1 (877) 407-4847

Interior Graphics/Art Credit: Sarah LaFayette

ISBN: 978-1-9822-4366-1 (sc)
ISBN: 978-1-9822-4367-8 (e)

Print information available on the last page.

Balboa Press rev. date: 03/06/2020

**BALBOA**.PRESS
A DIVISION OF HAY HOUSE

Betty Baba's eyes spring open just as the first rays of morning light enter her room. She takes just a moment noticing what a beautiful morning it is before launching herself out of bed.

Betty gobbles down a delicious breakfast surrounded by her family and thinks to herself, "My days are always so good when they start like this."

That was yummy. Thanks mom!" she says as she runs upstairs to put on her favorite outfit. Her red stripped shirt, green skirt with the bow, and super stomper mud boots. "Wow you look great! You don't need to change at all." She giggles to herself as she runs out to catch the bus.

Her mom yells, "Have a great day honey."
Betty yells back, "I will mom. I know I will. Love you."

Betty gets on the bus and sits next to her best buddy Derek Dog.

At the next stop, Dump the orange orangutan gets on the bus. Yelling "Move!" at a smaller student Dump sits in his usual seat. Betty and Derek are quiet while they watch Dump make everyone around him uncomfortable.

First he kicks the seat in front of him making a shy girl who Betty has never seen before cry out, "Ouch!" Then Dump steals an apple out of another student's backpack. Dump acts selfish and rude. Betty's face gets hot. She feels angry and sad at the way Dump is acting.

Betty stands up at the next stop. She wants to tell on Dump, but the driver sees her standing and orders her to get back to her seat. Looking at Derek as she sits down, he whispers, "At least he's not picking on us."

Betty tries to forget about Dump but inside she knows ignoring the problem won't solve anything.

As Betty and her classmates find their seats the teacher announces, "Class we have a new student. This is Maria Mouse." He gestures to the shy girl who was kicked on the bus. Everyone says, "Hello Maria." Everyone except Dump.

When Maria moves to sit down, Dump blocks her way. "There is no room for you in this class!" he tells her. "Stop goofing around Dump." Mr. Cat tells him.

Dump had kicked Maria, blocked her seat, and told her she was not welcome. Betty could feel her face getting hot again. She could tell how upset Maria was too. Betty really just wanted to yell at Dump. "But what good would that do?" she thought to herself, "He wouldn't listen."

Betty's perfect day was gone. She could not get rid of the terrible feeling in her stomach yet she still remembered to thank the bus driver for getting her home safely.

Over dinner that night Betty's mom asks "Is something bothering you honey?"
Betty tells her family about all the mean things she saw Dump do that day.
Betty's older sister says, "What do you care? You don't even know the new girl."
"Yeah, stay out of it. Dump is mean. Just be glad it isn't you," adds her little
brother.
Betty looks at them with tears in her eyes as her mother says, "I don't know
kids. Is that what you would want people to do if you were treated like that?"

Betty says, "Don't you think the new girls has the right to feel safe and be treated nicely?" Betty pushes her chair out and walks outside to sit on the front steps.

Betty's mom comes out and sits next to her. "I am proud of you honey" her mom says hugging her. "The fact you are still thinking about this and are asking for advice on how to make things better, shows me you have really good morals."

"It sounds like today was really hard, and I can tell you want to do the right thing. Do you have any ideas?" her mom asks. "No I don't. I am just so mad!" Betty says as she takes one deep breath and then another, "I just felt so helpless!" Betty takes another deep breath and her eyes widen, "Wait maybe I do have an idea. Thanks for listening mom."

There is no sun as Betty's eyes pop open the next morning. Betty is so excited for school she does not notice. She looks for her favorite outfit, but remembers it is in the wash. "No matter!" she thinks.

Before running out to catch the bus, Betty stops for a long hug from her mom and asks, "May I have an extra banana for my lunch?" "Sure honey." her mom says. "Love you!" they say to each other as Betty runs out the door.

When Betty gets on the bus she sits where Dump always sits. When Dump gets on the bus and sees Betty sitting in his usual seat, his face turns even more orange with anger than normal. "Move, you are sitting in my seat!" Dump scowls. "I know," Betty answers smiling, "I wanted to sit by you. Good morning."

Surprised, Dump sits down. Pulling the banana from her bag Betty says, "I brought you this." Frowning, Dump snatches the banana and eats it immediately. Through a full mouth he says "My mom likes to sleep really late, so I never get breakfast at home."

"That sounds hard." Says Derek Dog.
Embarrassed Dump kicks the seat in front of him. "Hey! No need to kick,"
Betty tells Dump. He looks at her still embarrassed. Maria hands back an
apple from her lunch sack. Dump grabs it and eats it too.

When they get to school Dump stands up and starts to leave. Betty asks, "Can I sit with you again tomorrow? I will bring another banana. I know I have a hard time when I haven't eaten." Dump shrugs, "OK."

"How did you know he was hungry?" Derek asks as they get off the bus. "I didn't. I just thought if I showed him some kindness first maybe he would be more kind." Turning to her new friends, Maria says, "Thank you. It is scary being the new kid. You are really brave. "

"No problem." Betty says. "It is hard, but sometimes the change that we want to see in the world has to start within ourselves!"

CPSIA information can be obtained
at www.ICGtesting.com
Printed in the USA
LVHW071737060420
652383LV00009B/570